HAPPILY
NEVER AFTER

PRANAVIKA
VIJAYARAGHAVAN

Contents

DEDICATED TO

My Beloved Sisters
Gyan & Kannamma,
Parents,
Grandparents
& Friends

ACKNOWLEDGEMENTS

I thank my dear sister Gyan
for her effort in
colouring all my illustrations
with patience

I thank my dear Vichu Bro
for seeding the idea of the
story in me that encouraged
me to develop the series

I
CLAP CLAP!

Once, there lived a rich family of 4 (Mr. Henry Poe, Mrs. Elliana Poe, Lily Poe and Tom Poe) in a large mansion. It was said that the mansion they owned, was the largest mansion ever! The mansion had uncountable number of rooms with each room containing a lot of cool features. Many people were very jealous of the Poe family.

One day, Lily ran to her parents' bedroom and she asked, "Mom, dad, can we go on a trip?".

"Why do you suddenly ask, dear?", asked Mrs. Poe.

"I dunno! I just felt like visiting someplace", replied Lily.

"Elliana, she is right. We've mostly never left home. We work from home and the kids are homeschooled too. She must've got bored staying inside the mansion all the time!", explained Mr. Poe.

"Well, ok then. Go inform Tom and we'll leave tomorrow. By the way, don't forget to pack, Lily!", announced Mrs. Poe.

"OK mom, thanks!", beamed Lily and dashed joyfully to her room.

The next day, the Poe family was ready to go on a 2 day trip to a nearby town. Tom, wore a backpack and had a luggage with him, Lily wore her backpack, had a luggage and their pet dog Sunny, in her arms. Mr. Poe was already waiting in the car for the rest of the family.

"MOM! LET'S GO! Dad's waiting in the car for us already. QUICK!", yelled Tom.

"Tom, its Ok!.", Lily said. "Mom, we're gonna sit in the car", she added.

"I. JUST. NEED. TO. GET. MY. MAKEUP. DONE!", grunted Mrs. Poe.

Tom and Lily strolled out into the lawn, with Sunny hopping beside them. Suddenly, a thought popped in Tom's mind- 'What if the house gets robbed? There's no safety. We can't trust the security, can we?'

"Tom, what happened?", asked Lily, and that is when he realised that his sister was already seated in the car. Tom sprinted through the lawn and joined Lily and Sunny in the car.

"Lily, we'll be gone for 2 days, right? We need protection for the house. And- OH MY GOSH- the security asked for a week off, remember, so there are chances of the house getting robbed!", exclaimed Tom.

"A housekeeper is perfect!", said Lily.

Just then, Mrs. Poe entered the car.

"Mom, we need a housekeeper!", shouted Tom.

"Why, Tom?", she asked.

"We need protection", said Lily.

"And the security asked for a week off, remember?", asked Tom.

"Nah, it's alright!", said Mr. Poe.

"Henry, actually, they're right. My friend Emily got robbed recently. You know her, don't ya Henry? Didn't care about the house and now she's paying for it!", informed Mrs. Poe.

"Well, in that case, I'll inform the housekeeping unit to send a housekeeper here. The key is under the welcome mat. We'll tell them", said Mr, Poe.

"LET'S GOOOOOOOOOOOOO!!!", hurried the kids.

And so, their car slowly came into motion and suddenly dashed out the gates and turned at the end of the street.

A few hours later, a tall girl with pale skin and long blonde hair tied in a ponytail, came closer to the mansion, lifted the welcome mat, her large, shiny, bright green eyes searched for the key. After a moment or so, she took the key in her hand that shimmered with lilac painted nails and opened the door with it.

"Woah" she gasped as she entered the large living area. She placed her violet bag on the couch and started exploring the mansion. She went up the stairs, out into the lawn, into the library and literally everywhere she could find.

A while later Lorea started to get hungry. She opened her bag, took a sandwich from it and munching, she explored some more. After devouring the sandwich with not even a single crumb left, she felt like washing her hands as they were all cheesy and sticky. She entered the vast kitchen and opened the kitchen tap.

"AAAAAAAAAHHHHHHHHH!!!!!!!!!!!!!!!!!!!", Lorea screamed. Instead of water, blood came out the tap. Panting, she closed the tap and taking a deep breath, she muttered, "It's just your imagination", and opened the tap again. But this time was no different. Again sparkling blood came out the tap. Astonished, Lorea ran out of the kitchen.

Then, she went to the entertainment room, sat on the couch and then, when she was about to turn on the TV, she noticed a note. Tucking a strand of blonde hair behind her ear, she took the note and read, "CLAP CLAP!". She clapped her hands twice and the lights turned off! Then, she clapped twice again and the lights turned on!

"WOW!", she whispered.

Lorea was watching a basketball match on the television to make herself feel better. She suddenly felt someone passing by her left side. She turned to see who it was and was in complete shock.

"AAAAAAAAAHHHHHHHHHH!!!!!!!!!!!!!!!!!!!!!", yelled Lorea. She saw a little girl wearing a white frock, with pale skin and red scratch marks on her soft and delicate hands. The girl's face was covered with shoulder length jet-black hair. Scared, Lorea turned towards the TV and turned left again, but there was no one. Lorea looked at the TV and this time felt someone standing towards her right corner. She turned right and saw the same little girl. Breathing heavily, she clapped twice to put the lights out, and a moment later, turned them back on. This time, there was no one in the room apart from Lorea.

"See, it's not real. It's just your imagination. It's ok Lorea!", she consoled herself.

A while later, Lorea became really hungry. Her stomach grumbling, she rose from the couch and walked into the kitchen. Lorea opened the fridge, but she saw nothing apart from fruits and veggies inside. She opened the cabinet and let out a deadly scream.

"AAAAAAAAAAAAAAAAAAAAAAAAAAAAAAAAAAHHHHHHHHHHHH!!!".

She saw an awful sight. Amidst all the spice boxes, there was a girl's pale head with black hair covering most of the face grinning at Lorea. Blood was dripping beneath the head. She immediately closed the cabinet, and slowly opened it again and was surprised to see just boxes filled with spices and cookies. The head wasn't there.

"Look it's nothing. You're imagining again!", Lorea said to herself.

Lorea walked up the stairs and into the dark master bedroom. She clapped twice and the lights turned on, 'clap clap' and the Air Conditioner turned on. Lying on the bed, she was thinking of all the incidents that had occurred.

"I have to go back to the housekeeping unit tomorrow and tell the manager to send someone else here. This place is creepy!", she thought.

Just then, Lorea heard a low eerie sound followed by 'Clap Clap'. The lights went out and the room turned extremely cold.

Lorea clapped twice and the room turned back to how it was earlier. 'Clap clap', she heard it again and the lights went out.

"What is this?", Lorea muttered and clapped twice again. This continued to happen a few more times and poor Lorea couldn't do anything and so she gave up. A few minutes later, the lights turned on by themselves.

Lying on the bed, was Lorea's body. Blood was splattered all over the white cotton bedsheets. Scratch marks were on her hands, and her head was nowhere to be found.

The next day, the mansion was very quiet. Not a single movement was detected. The day after that was the return of the Poe family.

The family had just entered the mansion, thinking that the housekeeper had left early. Suddenly, Tom asked, "Lily, is this yours?". He was holding a large sparkly violet bag.

"No Tom. It must be the housekeeper's. She must've forgotten it in a hurry", replied Lily.

Mr. and Mrs. Poe entered their bedroom, and what they saw made them freeze with horror. There it was, lying on the bed, the body of a girl, beheaded with blood splattered everywhere. But the thing that scared them to death was a little girl wearing a white frock with shoulder length jet-black hair munching on Lorea's hand. Frightened, Mr. and Mrs. Poe ran out of the room.

Meanwhile, Lily was roaming in the kitchen, looking for something to eat. She opened a cabinet.

"AAAAAAAAAAAHHHHHHHHHHHHHHHHH!!!!!!!!!!!", she bellowed.

Tom came running with Mr. and Mrs. Poe behind him.Lily was pointing to something. In the middle of boxes filled with yummy treats, there was a head. A head with long blonde hair tied into a neat, high pony tail. Its bright green eyrs looked deeply into theirs, its mouth stretched into an evil grin.

"YOU'RE NEXT!", they heard a voice and turned to see a girl wearing a white frock with shoulder length jet- black hair. She cackled loudly walking towards the scared family...

THE END

II

THE HAUNTED MANSION

In an abandoned street, there was a large mansion. A mansion, where nobody lived but rumours say that during 12-1 AM every day, passer-by see the lights flicker, shadows by the window and whispers and screams of a girl. But, the people who have entered the mansion die within 2 days. It is said that the mansion lures people in with something they like.

One night, a family of five were travelling through the street and suddenly, their car broke down.

"What Happened, Daddy?", asked Lia, the middle child.

"The Car broke down dear", Mr. Lynson sighed.

"Its 12 AM! Am getting sleepy! ", gasped Riya, the elder one.

"Can you fix it, Jarrod?", asked Mrs. Lynson.

"I don't think so, Shira!", he replied.

"Then, we'll go and search for a place to stay. Come on!", yelled Mia, the youngest.

The Sisters got down the car and walked on the road to find the place to stay on the night. The street was shockingly empty – no people, no houses, no vehicles, no plants, no trees – NOTHING!! Nothing except for a large mansion.

"Look Riya, a mansion!", pointed Lia, but Riya didn't listen. She was busy chatting with her friends on her phone.

"RIYA!", shouted Mia.

"I'll call you guys later", said Riya and stuffed her phone into her pocket, "Yeah What?", she asked rudely to her sisters.

"Look!", said the girls pointing at the mansion.

"WOAH! And the lights are on too. LET'S GO!", bellowed Riya with excitement and ran towards the mansion. An Old woman came out when the girls knocked and rattled the gates with happiness. She looked very old, wrinkled, short and seemed disturbed and annoyed.

"What do you want?", she asked in a firm voice.

"Um-Our-Car-er…………broke d-down. C-can….", stammered Mia, she was always terrified to talk to strangers.

"Our Car broke down. Can we please stay here for one night", asked Riya.

"How many people?", the old lady asked.

"F-f-five!".

"Here's the key. I'm going out to a friend's place for an emergency. DON'T LOOSE THE KEY", she said mysteriously and limped away.

"Thank you so much!", Lia yelled after her.

Mia called Mr. and Mrs. Lynson to inform the news. They were very happy to hear this and they both strolled through the street to the mansion.

The mansion looked really beautiful. It was very large and it had a garden that had trees filled with juicy fruits, vines, creepers, plants and colourful flowers. It even had a large fountain in which the water shimmered and sparkled in the bright moon light.

The main door of the house was even a bigger surprise. The door has a carved image of a mother, father and 3 girls just like Lynsons. They thought it was the old lady's family.

Riya unlocked the door with the key and entered the house. Inside, they saw a very heart warming, welcoming sight. The house looked so neat and well decorated. The family admired the vintage look of the house and the antique decorated pieces.

It had a large diner table with all their favourite dishes. The Lynsons first thought that it was strange to see only their favourite food but then convinced that it was a coincidence. They feasted on the food as they were exhausted due to their travel. After devouring, they climbed up a large staircase inside the mansion to explore.

They found 3 bedrooms, a large library, an old storage room and an entertainment room.

Riya loved reading, so she explored the books inside the library. It had a books of all genres, sizes and languages.

"WOAH!", gasped Riya.

She took a book from a random shelf and started to read, but didn't find it appealing. Then she took another book from a different shelf.

"The Haunted Mansion! Cool!", said Riya, as she opened the book and sat on the couch to read it:

"In an abandoned street, there was a large mansion. A mansion, where nobody lived but rumours say that during 12-1 AM every day, passer-by see the lights flicker, shadows by the window and whispers and screams of a girl. But the people who have entered the mansion die within 2 days. It is said that the mansion lures people in with something they like!"

Suddenly, the lights started flickering and the room got cold. Riya heard a little girl's whispering, but couldn't make any meaning out of it. The light went out! She couldn't handled the chillness and started shivering. Riya grabbed her phone from her pocket, "It's 12:40 AM , the story! ", she gasped and turned on her phone's torchlight, "AAAAAAAAAAAAHHHHHHHHHHH!!!!!!!!!!!!!!!!".

The other Lynsons were sleeping and poor Riya didn't know that the walls were sound proofed. But, what did she see?

A little girl holding an knife and floating above Riya's head and when Riya saw her, the girl gave an evil laugh, started whispering in an unknown language and suddenly dropped down next to Riya.

"Hello Riya! Come on, Let's Float together! Let's Float together. Come on, Let's Float together! Let's Float together. LET'S FLOAT TOGETHER, Riya!", the girl yelled........

"Wh-Wh-Who are you? How do you know my name?", Riya shuddered. The girl didn't reply, but cackling, she started cornering Riya.

"AAAAAAAAAAAAHHHHHHHHHHHH!!!!!!!!!!!!!!!!", Riya closed her eyes with fear.

Riya slowly opened her eyes and realized that she was at home. She was glad that everything was a dream but it felt so realistic that she was not sure.

"No, nothing like that happened", said Mia.

"Looks like you've had a royal dream. Living in a mansion and all", joked Lia.

"I AM BEING SERIOUS!", Riya shouted at her sisters and stomped back to her room.

"No! This is not happening!", she exclaimed, horror-struck to see a book titled , 'THE HAUNTED MANSION' on her bed.

The moment Riya picked up the book and started reading it, her eyes widened:

❧

"If you are reading this then it means that you are very lucky. If you remember something that others don't, you are special! SO FLOAT WITH US!".

❧

Then, the door locked, the lights started to flicker and the room turned very cold.

Riya heard a voice:
"HELLO RIYA, COME ON, LET'S FLOAT TOGETHER!".......................

ജ

THE END

III
THE BOOK

"Alex, Look what I found!", yelled Allen.

"What's that? It's creepy Allen, Where did you find it?", asked Alex.

"It was in a old pile of presents, Let's open it", suggested Allen.

"OK, little brother. Hand it over, let me see!".

Allen gave the book to Alex. The book was old, brown, damaged and the front cover had a six-sided star with a skull in front. Alex carefully opened it.

"Hey, I'll read", insisted Allen, grabbing the book and smiled. "OK!", he read:

"Readers beware! This book takes you to a world which you'll love. But be careful, because when things change, you might not enjoy your fate".

"Creepy!", chuckled Alex.

"Wait, there is more. **To begin, touch the star below**", Allen read.

Below the text, there was a six-sided star.

"Wait, am thirsty. I'll be back. We'll start together, Ok!", said Alex and walked out of the room.

"ALEX!", Allen Screamed.

Alex dropped the glass of water and ran to his room but it was too late. Alex was gone.

"No!", sobbed Alex holding the book.

Present day:

"Alex, its been a month!", Mrs. Zin said.

"I know, Mom, but he was the best!", said Alex tears falling down his eyes.

"Go to School, Make new friends. Enjoy, It's ok!", she replied.

"No, its not. I don't know anyone at school. At least, I would have had Allen, but......",he started sobbing.

"It's your first day, you'll get used to it", said Mrs. Zin patting his shoulder.

Alex wiped his eyes, mounted his bag on his shoulder, got up and went outside. After waiting for a few minutes, the school bus arrived. Silently, he got on it and sat on a deserted seat. A while later, a girl with bushy brown hair stood next to him.

"Is this seat occupied?", she asked.

"No, you can sit", said Alex.

"Thanks!", she chuckled and sat next to Alex, "You are new? I've never seen you before", she said.

"Yeah!", said Alex.

"I'm Avery!", she said.

"I'm Alex, nice to meet you!", he said gazing into her bright blue eyes.

"You remind me of my brother. Big blue eyes, bushy brown hair, your laughter. It's just like Allen", said Alex.

" Where's he? Allen", Avery asked.

"Well, he's no more!", said Alex, a single tear rolling down his eye.

"Oh, I'm sorry Alex. Glad I look like him", Avery said, her eyes filled with tears.

"Hey, it's ok. We were a little careless and as the elder one I should've been more responsible. Well, it was my fault", he said.

"How'd it happen?", asked Avery.

"Well,...", before Alex could start, the bus came to a halt and all the kids noisily rushed out.

"I'll tell ya later", he said and they got down too.

"LITTLETON INTERNATIONAL!", sighed Avery, "It's actually not that bad. It's just that, you can't play, you can't talk unless you're spoken to, you shouldn't backtalk, you can't shout, no running in the corridors, you have to sit where you're assigned to sit and probably just a thousand more rules. That's it!", she said.

"OH NO! What have I gotten myself into?", Alex gasped.

"Relax. I was just kidding! It's really fun! You can talk, play, sit wherever you want, but you better listen to class. That's it!", she laughed.

They entered the great door to see loads of busy students hurrying in the corridors, running up and down the stairs.

"Here, this way", Avery pulled the confused Alex into a corridor.

"28, 29, 30, 31, 32, 33. Here, class 34! 8A. Our class, remember this Ok?", she said.

Inside, the class looked totally new and different from the rest of the school. The bright white of the corridors were replaced with a pale pastel blue. The soft board had a picture of Avery titled 'STUDENT OF THE MONTH'. The benches had 2 chairs and 3 benches were connected to form triangles in each corner. The books were neatly arranged and perfectly labelled on the shelves.

"What's that?", Alex pointed to a dash in the place of the sixth period in the time table.

"Oh, yeah. During one period every day, you get to do whatever you want- talking playing, reading a book, sleeping. You can even hang out of class, go and have a walk, go to the library, play soccer, basketball or tennis. It's called the free period", Avery explained.

"Are we allowed to eat during the fun period?", Alex joked.

"Actually, yeah!", chuckled Avery.

"For real?", asked Alex.

"Yeah!", Avery said and they both laughed.

They both took a seat in the centre and just then, their teacher, Miss Rosalina entered.

"GOOD MORNING, MISS LINA!", the students greeted, very loudly.

"Good morning guys!", she greeted them back, "Now, where is Alex Zin?", she asked.

"Yes, Miss Lina?" Alex stood up.

"Ah, this is your new classroom. Feel free to ask anything to any of your friends. Oh, and, students, it's your responsibility to make Alex feel comfortable", informed Miss Lina.

"Sure, Miss Lina!", the other students replied.

It was the fun period! The class was almost empty as kids rushed to the library to read. A few athletic ones with loads of energy dashed to the soccer and basketball courts. The lazy students rushed to the canteen to gobble up some tasty hamburgers and chocolate muffins. There were pupils almost everywhere apart from their respective classrooms! The only ones left in the classroom were Alex and his new friend Avery.

"I'm bored!", sighed Avery.

"Hey, I've a book to read. It's quite creepy!", suggested Alex.

"Ok! Let's read it", said Avery.

Alex opened the book and started to read:

"Readers beware! This book takes you to a world which you'll love. But be careful, because when things change, you might not enjoy your fate. To begin, touch the star below!"

"On 3, together!", said Avery.

"One, two, three!", they touched the star.

There was a bright flash of light and when Alex opened his eyes, he found himself in a small island and Avery next to him.

"Where are we?", asked Avery rubbing her eyes.

"ALLEN, ALLEN!", Alex yelled.

After this, the place changed completely. The small, beautiful island turned into a large old mansion. There was a board in front which read 'MANSION OF THE DEMON'.

"Should we go in?", Avery suggested.

"Yeah, we should", Alex said and started running towards the mansion's large door.

"Alex, what are you – ", Avery panted.

"Avery, just follow me. I'll explain later", Alex yelled.

Avery sprinted really hard to catch up with Alex. She had no idea of what Alex was doing, but just trusted him and followed him. Alex stopped very abruptly once he reached the door which made Avery bump her forehead into him.

"OUCH!", she shrieked.

"Oopsie Sorry!", Alex replied.

"It's fine".

They looked at the mansion's humungous door and gasped in awe. It was a large wooden door which had a very unique scene carved on it. The carvings depicted a demon king seated on a throne with deadly-looking guards on his left side and people trapped in cages (prisoners) on his right side. The door had a large golden knob on the centre of its right edge. Alex turned the knob carefully to reveal a long hall with a throne situated in the centre of the farthest corner. They entered the hall and the door slammed shut behind them.

Alex turned to look behind. Just then,

"AAAAAAAAAAHHHHHHHHHHH!!!!!!!!!!", Avery screamed.

Alex turned to see huge skeletons with a golden armour and big spears in their hand. Their eyes looked like red lasers and their jaws broke into a creepy smile. They stood on the left side.

"The Guards!", Avery gasped.

There was a white curtain on the right side of the throne splattered with blood. With a screech, it opened. And inside was Alex's beloved brother trapped inside a large cage.

"ALLEN!" It's you! I've missed you!", Alex cried.

"The Prisoner, it's … Allen! But you said he died Alex. What's going on?", Avery asked.

"It's the book – ", Alex started, "About a month ago, he found a book. We opened it. I was thirsty so I went to fetch some water. Allen touched the star in the book and when I came back, he was gone. Everyone thought he was dead but I always believed he was still there. You reminded me of Allen. I really wanted to see my brother, so I came here and what I thought was true, he is here".

"Why did you bring me here?", asked Avery.

"I couldn't do this alone, Avery. I'm Sorry!", said Alex.

"Allen, Let's go!", said Alex running towards the cage.

Neither did Allen reply, nor did he move.

"Allen, come!", Alex said again, this time a little nervous.

They heard a loud rumbling noise. The floor beneath the throne cracked open and Allen emerged from underneath. The big blue eyes he had turned red and his laughter no longer sounded like a little boy's. Huge horns emerged from his head. The Allen inside the cage was not a real person but just a statue. It was placed there as a decoy. The Demonic Allen sat on the throne.

"Alex, Allen's not a prisoner. He is the DEMON!", gasped Avery.

"My dear brother", Allen boomed in a loud voice. "I've always been waiting for you. Let's rule the world together. Come on, Alex. Join me".

"No, Alex!", yelled Avery.

"Oh Alex, I never found the book under the pile of old presents. Avery gave it to me", chuckled Allen.

"What!", Alex gasped.

"By the way, Avery is the prisoner here. The Demon who ruled previously sent her to look for a person to take the role of the demon. She thought I was perfect. And now I sent her to find you,

Avery can shapeshift, you know", Allen explained.

"Alex, do you remember my picture titled 'STUDENT OF THE MONTH'. Sorry, it's not me. Her name is Emily. I killed her so I can take her shape and get disguised as a normal human", cackled Avery.

"Let's rule together, Alex. Come on!", Allen smiled.

"NO!", refused Alex.

"Sure?", asked Allen.

"Yes! I don't want to rule the world. I just want my brother back!", said Alex firmly.

"I'm sorry! That's not possible", said Allen.

"Then I'm leaving!", Alex said.

"You can't", said Avery, "There is only one option left".

"What is it?", asked Alex.

"You have to die!", laughed Allen.

Alex turned to run, but Avery threw a wand to Allen which he pointed at Alex. A spark hit Alex and he fell on the shiny floor, dead.

"Avery, turn into Alex and go live on Earth. I've set you free!", commanded Allen.

"THANK YOU, YOUR MAJESTY", chucked Avery and turned into Alex within a second, with a large, murderous smile on Avery's face who now look like the Demon king's brother.

THE END

IV
DREAM COME TRUE

Selena was always passionate about writing stories. She has always dreamt of becoming a big, famous author. She never got bored of writing stories. When people asked her why she was obsessed with reading and writing stories, Selena would reply "From my childhood I've been listening and reading. Whether they are happy stories, fairy tales, tragical stories about dystopian future or scary stories, I love to listen to them. Slowly, I got the interest of writing stories. If I become a successful author, it would be a dream come true for me!".

Even though Selena had published quite a few books, she was never satisfied. She always wanted to do better.

On her 13th birthday, Selena's parents organised a secret birthday party. Selena was surprised to see all her friends and family waiting for her. After the party was over, Selena's hazel brown eyes gazed at the gifts. She opened the presents one by one, but none of the gifts impressed her. There was one present left, it had a note, but no name mentioned. Curiously, Selena opened the note.

Dear Selena,

This gift has the ability to make your dream come true, but use it wisely.

Beware, because the moment the magic starts working, something will be taken.

Something precious....

"OOH!", chuckled Selena as she took the gift carefully on her hands as if it was fragile.

Glancing at a shiny wrapper, she unwrapped slowly revealing a new, elegant pen. It's metal body glimmered with a silvery blue sparkle. She just loved it! Selena immediately grabbed a piece of paper to test the pen. She wrote '*Selena*', It glowed brightly on the paper.

Selena felt as if someone hit her head with a hard substance. She touched her forehead groaning in pain. But ignoring the pain, she thought of writing incidents and stories with her brand-new pen. Selena got the perfect idea too! Let's take a look at her first story with her new pen:

୪୨

There once lived a girl called Maria. Her parents were planning on buying a new house. Maria was very excited! After a long of waiting, the big day finally arrived. They packed all their belongings and shifted to their new home. The house had beautiful chandelier hanging on the centre of the ceiling in the living room. It was made of glass and precious stones and crystals. But there was a huge problem about it. Every time, it was turned on, it flickered a lot, which made the scene more disturbing and annoying. But Maria thought that paranormal activities had been occurring in the new house. One day, Maria was sitting in the living room, watching TV. Suddenly, the chandelier started flickering. Scared, Maria turned it off. Still, with no electricity, the chandelier flickered. Astonished, Maria took a notebook tore a paper from it and scribbled something. 'BOOM!", the chandelier exploded!

THE END
୪୨

Selena read through her story again, but she was not that happy with what she has written. Her creativity level had clearly decreased compared to the other stories she had written.

Just then, Selena got a phone call. She answered it hurriedly. Her eyes widened as she heard the news. Her friend Sally died due to the explosion of a chandelier. There was a note in which the word 'PARANORMAL' was written. Selena immediately rushed to Sally's house. That house looked just like Selena's imaginary new home in her story. Was this a coincidence? Or was there something more to it? Selena was confident to find out.

She went back home and sat in her room, thinking. "What did the note say?", Selena tried to recall.

"Something about magic?", Selena thought.

She took the crushed note from the bin and read through it again. "OH, NO! Sally!", she exclaimed.

Suddenly, something struck in Selena's mind. She grabbed her notebook and wrote '**A+ in English test**' with the magic pen.

The next day, when Selena arrived at school, her English teacher had a surprise for her. "You got A+!", she said.

Slowly Selena started to write incidents with the magic pen. But, as time passed by Selena felt like she ran out of ideas easily and her headaches kept getting worse. Little by little, greed took over Selena. She wrote an incident: '**Selena is the best author ever. Her stories are famous worldwide. She has a lot of awards!**'.

The moment she wrote that she felt a deep pain in her head, but she ignored it and waited for the magic to happen. A few days later, many people and famous authors invited Selena to parties and presented her with awards and trophies for her stories. She was a successful author!

But all the stories she wrote were becoming worse. The little girl Selena who wrote extra ordinary stories which was even though known by only a few, was praised due to the way it was written. Now, author Selena's stories had become much more boring! What happened to her? She thought it had something to do with that magic pen.

She opened her laptop, went online and typed 'Weird Birthday presents!', but she didn't get proper results. She typed 'Mysterious presents with note'. There was an article, it was about a girl named Olivia, who was a wild life photographer. She was presented with a camera on her birthday. There was a note that said:

'Dear Olivia,

This gift has the ability to make your dream come true, but use it wisely.

Beware, because the moment the magic starts working, something will be taken.

Something precious....'

Olivia's dream was to display all her pictures in popular magazines, books and even in museums. But, as she started to use new camera, the clarity in her picture started decreasing. Every time she photographed something, she felt strange. Then she figured out that 'Something precious' was taken from Olivia. Her photography skills were gone. The precise timing and angle she had as a regular photographer had become worse and she could never achieve her dream.......

Selena thought "But, I've become a famous author. My dream came true". But there was one thing Selena couldn't figure out. What precious thing was taken from her? How could she find out? Suddenly, she got an idea!

"I should meet Olivia!", she gasped. Selena searched over the internet for Olivia's address and when she found it without wasting any time, she took off.

Selena reached the photographer's house from the outside, it looked like a wooden cabin. The wooden walls were painted with a shade of warm white. The door was bright white with a brass knob in the corner. Olivia had grown lots of colourful plants which were used as decoration around the house. Selena knocked the door. A girl opened the door. She was thin and had short, red hair. Her eyes shined a brilliant green, her lips were scarlet and she had a freckled oval face.

"Hi dear, am Olivia Max, what do you want?", she asked Selena in a calm, sweet voice.

"Hi, am Selena May. I want to ask you about something", Selena tried to sound as polite as possible.

"You're SELENA, as in author Selena?", Olivia asked awestruck.

"Yes!"

"Come in, Come in!".

Selena entered Olivia's house. It looked beautiful. Olivia signalled Selena to sit. "Do you want cookies?", she asked.

"Yes please!", replied Selena.

Olivia entered the kitchen and came back with a plate filled with delicious cookies. She gently placed it on the table and sat next to Selena on the sofa.

"Yes, what do you want to ask?", said Olivia curiously.

"I read your article. The one that was posted online about the magic camera. Do you want the camera and the note?", Selena ended with a question.

"Yes, it's in my cupboard. Just a minute", Olivia said and rushed to her bedroom.

She had a big camera in one hand and tiny note in the other. She kept the camera on the table and gave the note to Selena. Selena glanced at the camera and then carefully looked at the note. It looked exactly like the one Selena had received, the paper's texture, the colour of the pen ink, the colour of the paper and most importantly the hand writing. It was all the same!

"Why are you so interested in this? Are you planning on writing a story based on this idea?", Olivia asked.

"No! Olivia, the same thing is happening to me!", Selena said.

"WHAT?", Olivia was shocked. Selena took her pen and a note from her pocket.

"Almost anything I write with this pen comes true!", Selena said.

"Almost, what do you mean? Is there something that didn't happen?", asked Olivia.

"Yes!", said Selena, and munching on a cookie she continued "I wanted to test the pen, so I wrote a tragical event about two friends dying due to an explosion. That did not happen!".

"OK, WAIT! What was taken from you?", Olivia asked.

"That's why I'm here. I couldn't figure it out! I need your help", said Selena.

"Ok! By the way I have a second batch of cookies in the oven. Tell me if you want some", said Olivia.

"No, Thankyou though. I really need your help to find what is taken from me", informed Selena.

"So, what is taken must be something related to the gift and definitely something that you will need. For example, I was a photographer and I was gifted with a camera. I will need photography skills, which was taken from me. You are an author and you were gifted with a pen. What will you need for writing great stories? Um- ", Olivia was deep in thinking.

Then, Olivia asked, "How do you feel about the stories you've written with the pen?".

"Er- To be honest, am not that satisfied. I run out of ideas easily and even my friends said that the stories I've written recently are boring", Selena answered.

"Selena, I think I know what is taken from you!"

"What is it, Olivia? Tell me please!", begged Selena.

"Your creativity and imagination! As an author, you need to be creative and imaginative enough to write a story. But I don't understand one thing! How come every single thing came true, except one?".

Selena had doubted this too. Just then, they heard a loud beeping noise coming from the kitchen.

"Oh no, the cookies!", Olivia screamed as she ran to the kitchen but it was too late.

"BOOM!", the whole cabin exploded.

Selena and Olivia's body was found by the cops the next day. But it looks like the incident was true after all.

THE END

V
HOCUS POCUS

Carol and Chris were twins. They loved each other so much and always supported each other. No matter what happened, they were inseparable. But there is always one thing about twins – they are different from each other in every possible way, based on likes and dislikes.

Carol liked to sing but Chris liked to dance. Carol played the guitar but Chris played the piano. Carol and Chris were always like this, which gave them a big advantage. While Carol sang, Chris danced. While Carol played the guitar, Chris played the piano.

Everybody could tell that they were twins, even if a stranger met them for the first time, he would surely know. That's because they shared the same neat, red hair and olive-green eyes. But Chris was a teeny bit taller than Carol. They both had the same pinkish skin and freckle and the same light pink lips. Carol had a wider smile while Chris smiled with his mouth closed.

They've studied together in the same school from the beginning. Almost everybody in the school knew them.

It was a very exciting day for the twins. It was their best friend Harry's birthday. Harry was having a birthday party for the first time and his parents allowed him to invite only a few friends. And, of course, Harry invited Carol and Chris.

It was just morning, but they hadn't bought Harry a present yet. They rushed to their dad and asked him to take them to a gift shop. Their dad agreed and they got ready while their dad Mr. Jeff was cleaning the car. A few minutes later, the twins entered the car with their dad.

"Carol, what are you going to buy for Harry?", asked Chris.

"I don't know! You?", replied Carol.

"I am not sure too!", answered Chris.

"What does he like?", asked Carol.

"BOOKS!", gasped Chris.

"Um, that's an option. Ooh, what about a new lamp for his desk. He has always wished for one!", gasped Carol.

"Kids, we're here!", said Mr. Jeff.

They entered the shop but the moment they were inside, the twins ran in different directions.

Mr. Jeff waited near the cashier counter. After about 30 minutes, Carol came back. She had a new shiny desk lamp and a ceramic mug that read 'Harry and the twins'.

"Wow, Carol! Harry will surely like your gifts", Mr. Jeff exclaimed.

"Dad, Is Chris not here yet?", asked Carol.

"No, maybe he's looking for something", Mr. Jeff said.

On the other hand:

Chris was walking through an aisle filled with antique pieces. He saw vases and cups that had a simple floral pattern. He saw lamps and marble jars. He had already got Harry's present. It was a novel written by Harry's most favourite author. And it was a special copy too (signed by the author herself)! But Chris wanted something to decorate Carol and his room, so he got a tiny statue of twins holding hands (representing Chris and Carol). When he was about to leave the aisle, something caught Chris attention. He saw a 11-inch-long wooden wand. Chris was always a big fan of magic and fantasy, so he decided to buy it. He walked back to the cash counter with his arms filled with stuff.

"OMG Chris! What's all this?", asked a surprised Carol.

"This is for Harry!", said Chris giving the book to the cashier.

"This is for our room, Carol!", he said giving over the statue.

"That's so sweet!", commented Mr. Jeff.

"And this, is for me!", he said holding up the wand.

"Cool!", gasped Carol.

Later that day:

The twins got down the car parked in front of Harry's house. It was completely decorated for the party.

"Chris, do you know that there is a pool in the backyard! I saw it the day I came here to do our science project with Harry", Carol said excitedly.

There was a small girl standing in front of the door. She had a notebook and a pen with her checking if every person who was about to enter the house were invited. Carol & Chris walked to the front door which presents in their arms.

"Hello, am Charlotte Warmhill, Harry's sister. Please give me your name so I can check if you are invited. Wait, are you twins?", the girl asked in a sweet voice.

"Yes, we're twins. I am Carolina Jeff".

"And I am Christopher Jeff".

"Hey guys! Am sorry, you are not invited", sighed Charlotte.

"Can I check?", asked Chris.

"Here", said Charlotte giving the book to Chris.

Chris checked through the list and turned over the page and saw their names under the title 'Special guests'.

"Here! See", he said giving it back to the birthday boy's sister.

"Oh! Looks like everybody is here. Let's get inside", said Charlotte leading the twins inside.

The house looked so beautiful on the inside. It was perfect for the party. Everybody was waiting for the birthday boy to get ready. The twins wanted to meet their friend, so they asked Mr. Warmhill if they could see Harry. They quickly climbed up the stairs and knocked on Harry's door.

"Yes! Please come in", they heard a voice.

They opened the door and Harry was really glad to see his best friends.

"GUYS! Hello!", he gasped with happiness.

The twins entered Harry's room. The room mostly had the colours – red and black.

"Harry, I didn't know you have a sister", said Carol.

"You said you've visited him. How come you never met Charlotte?", asked Chris.

"My mom had taken Charlotte to the park that day. They arrived an hour later after Carol left", explained Harry.

"Oh!", understood Chris.

"By the way, open the presents!", smiled Carol giving the presents to Harry.

Harry open the presents one by one and was delighted with everything his friends had got him.

"Hey, I've something to show you Harry!", said Chris as he took a small, but long box from his pocket. He opened the box and inside it was the wand that Chris had bought from the shop. There was a note too. Carol took the note and read it loudly.

'Say Hocus Pocus and let the magic begin! This is a magician's biggest gift'

"Should we try it?", asked Harry.

"Sure! What do we do?", asked Chris.

"Um-make Harry invisible but bring him back!", said Carol.

"Ok!", said Chris holding the wand at its edge and pointed it's tip on Harry, he said, "Hocus Pocus, Make Harry Warmhill invisible!".

A blue spark erupted from the wand and shot at Harry. Slowly, Harry started disappearing.

"Woah! So cool!", said Harry as he saw himself in the mirror.

Now, Harry was completely invisible!

"Harry, where are you?", asked Carol.

There was no reply, no movement, NOTHING!

"HARRY! YOU THERE?", yelled Chris.

Harry didn't answer!

Panicked, Carol grabbed the wand from Chris and said "Hocus Pocus, Make Harry Warmhill visible again!". She pointed the magic wand in all directions. Suddenly they saw something on the floor. Chris touched the red liquid splattered all over the floor. BLOOD! Slowly, Harry's body appeared. He was lying on the floor motionless! HARRY WAS LYING DEAD!

"Nooooo! HARRY!", yelled Carol.

"This is not supposed to happen. I am sorry!", Chris said silently.

Hearing a lot of noise Charlotte and Mrs. Warmhill walked up the stairs and opened the door. They saw their dear Harry lying dead and his two best friends crying silently beside him.

"HARRY!", screamed Charlotte.

"Kids, What – How? Please leave!", said Mrs. Warmhill.

Carol and Chris walked out and down the stairs. "The Party's Cancelled!", sobbed Carol.

All the people waiting groaned and the crowd slowly dispersed.

Carol and Chris walked all the way home, their eyes filled with tears.

"What happened?", asked Mrs. Jeff.

"Mom, the wand! It KILLED Harry!", wept Carol.

"I have to go the shop now", Chris said, determined.

"I'll come too", said Carol.

They rushed to the shop and asked the cashier if she knew something about the wand.

"No, it's just a toy wand. It glows when you say Hocus Pocus", she replied confused.

With no hope left, the twins were about to leave the shop, just then:

"Kids!", an old voice called them.

They turned to see an old man with a long beard. He smiled at them, but when he looked at Chris's face, for a while he froze with horror!

"You, bought the wand! What happened?", he asked curiously.

"You know about the wand?", Chris asked.

"Yes! But not many knows history. Don't worry! I do!", he grinned.

"Can you tell us?", asked Carol.

"Come to my cottage. It's nearby only. Just follow me", he said walking out of the shop.

Curiously, the twins followed the old man. It was just a five-minute walk from the store. The cottage was very old and was covered with cob webs. The old man opened the door. All around the cottage was lot of chemicals and apparatus.

"Excuse me, are you a scientist?", asked Carol.

"No! but I like science so I just do some experiments and a few tests and all that!", he replied.

"Cool! What's your name?", asked Chris.

"Ho-Sorry, Harold!", he replied.

"Ok! Tell us about the magic wand", Chris and Carol asked sitting on the floor, while Harold sat on a comfortable rocking chair and started narrating the story.

છ

"About eight decades ago, there lived a twin pair named Hocus and Pocus. They were inseparable twins but they had a tragic story. Both their parents died when they were young and the twins only had enough money to buy a small cottage to live in. But Hocus's dream was to create the world's most powerful wand that could grant anything anyone asked for! Even though Pocus liked his brother a lot, he always opposed this idea. He thought it might go wrong or put his twin's life in danger but Hocus was very stubborn and didn't want to give up. He tried a lot of attempts until one day he finally succeeded. He created a 11-inch-long wooden wand, and he wanted to test it on himself. Pocus was scared that it might affect his twin and without any thought told Hocus to test it on Pocus. Hocus didn't want to test it on his brother, but was left with no choice. With teary eyes he pointed the wand at his brother and said the magical words that denoted all their bond 'HOCUS POCUS!', he cried. A blue spark shot at Pocus which covered him in a weird bubble, but slowly Pocus turned unconscious and a while later, he died! After the death of his beloved brother, Hocus disappeared, but people gave the wand to an antique shop and the gifts shop owner bought it as a display for the antique's aisle. Nobody has seen Hocus. He could be alive or he could be dead! Nobody knows".

"What do we do now?", Carol asked.

"Do you have the wand?", Harold asked.

"Yes!", replied Chris.

"Give it to me", cackled old Harold.

Chris took the wand from his pocket and gave it to the old man. Harold examined it with carefully but with an evil grin, he pointed it at Carol and said "HOCUS POCUS!".

A blue spark shot at her and she was covered in a big bubble.

"CAROL!", Chris screamed, "I know who you are! You are HOCUS! You killed your brother but you lived all this while as Harold. Why did you do this to Carol?".

"You killed a poor little boy for your testing. That was your fault and now you have to feel the pain!", Hocus chuckled.

"Oh! You are brilliant too!", he commented.

"What are you going to do now?", asked Chris.

"Oh, am going to kill you too!", said Hocus and killed Chris the same way as Carol.

The wand was repacked and kept back at the shop whenever somebody bought it, they were always killed by HOCUS.

THE END

THIS IS NOT

THE END

UNTIL NEXT TIME

CREDITS

KNOW YOUR AUTHOR

Pranavika is 13 year old little angel for her parents Vijayaraghavan & Kayalvizhi.
Ever smiling Pranavika is a creative and multi-talented kid.
She discovered herself as a child author at the age of 9.
Her journey started with short stories further which she extended her genre to fictional thrillers.
She has also narrated her own stories in different podcast platforms.'

www.ingramcontent.com/pod-product-compliance
Lightning Source LLC
Chambersburg PA
CBHW040859110726
48005CB00001B/130